Izzy Gizmo

and the Invention Convention

Written by Pip Jones • Illustrated by Sara Ogilvie

PEACHTREE

ATLANTA

IZZY GIZMO and Fixer were making a racket
inventing a So-Sew to fix Grandpa's jacket, when

DING

DONG

DOINK!

went the bell on the door, and a golden
note fluttered down to the floor.

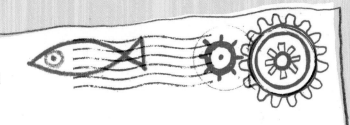

From the desk of Mick Marvel
General Secretary • Genius Guild

Ms. Gizmo,

We've heard you're a whiz with invention,
so you MUST come to our annual convention!
Arrive Thursday at noon. I do hope you're free.

Sincerely, Mick Marvel (Please RSVP)

Izzy gasped as the So-Sew started to jerk.
"Me?! My inventions—they don't always work!"
"Nonsense!" said Grandpa.

So, the very next day,
Izzy packed up her tools and they went on their way.

Over fields, hills, and waves,

they went mile after mile,

and followed a map 'til they reached...

Technoff Isle!

"Welcome, Inventors! Now, meet the Professor.
She wants you to make a machine to impress her.

If you place first with the thing that you build,
we'll make you a member of the Genius Guild!

Izzy Gizmo?

Will Digg?

Maximilian Spout?

Please reply 'here!' when your name is called out.

Abi von Lavish?

And Gillian Din?

PARP!

Everyone's here!
Very good. Let's BEGIN."

Abi von Lavish's bench was pristine.
She was already building a shiny machine.

"This thing's going to make heaps of sparkling jewels! Oh dear! Tell me Izzy, are those things your...

tools?!"

"Come on, Fixer!" said Izzy. "This couldn't be finer.
See my plan? It's a robotic fashion designer!

It'll be SO impressive: **The Magnifi-Style**.
But we need some supplies. I'll be back in a while!"
Izzy dashed to the cog store! But to her despair...

Abi von Lavish was already there.

Izzy rushed to the wire shed and looked on the shelf but Abi said, "Sorry, I need these myself."

Fixer flew off to fetch fan belts and wheels.
"Too late!" Abi smirked as she turned on her heels.

"I must get to work on my awesome design.
By this time tomorrow, THAT PRIZE WILL BE MINE!"

"What NOW?" Izzy groaned. "What else can we make?
A big **Bake-O-Copter** for delivering cake?
A **Night-Time-Erizer** for turning off lights?
An **Automa-Stretchy** for pulling up tights?!"

"Oh, Izzy!" smiled Grandpa. "Great inventors produce machines that can really be put to good use."

"You're right," Izzy sighed.

From behind came a CLUNK!

"My drill's busted!" called Abi.
"Take it out with the junk."

"Are all these tools broken?" Izzy gaped in dismay.
"You could mend them! You don't have to throw them away."

Then—PING! "Fixer! Quick! I've got a
new plan!

Bring those tools over here!" Izzy yelled as she ran.
"We'll make an invention to fix up this lot!

We might not have much, but we'll use
what we've got."

They both worked like crazy, all through the night,
and finally finished at dawn's twinkling light.

"I do hope it works, it was
quite problematic.

Presenting the
Tool-Fix-Recycle-O-Matic!

Let's test it," said Izzy, as she flicked the "ON" switch...

But, oh dear! The contraption did nothing but twitch.

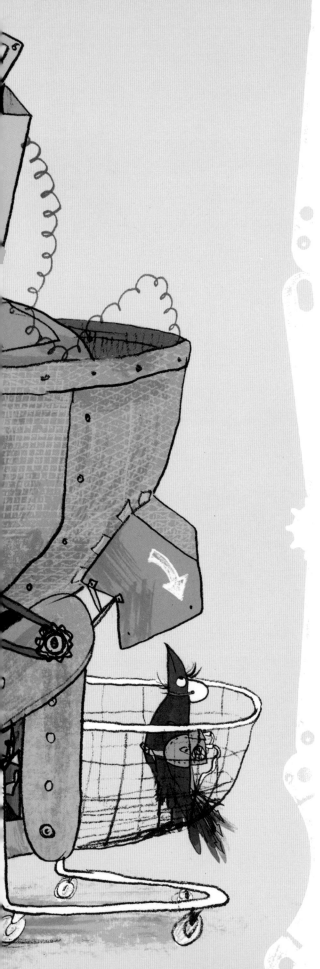

"ARGH! I've been wiring these plugs for an hour,
but Abi von Lavish has sapped all the power.
And now look! That thingummyjig's on the blink.
We have to do something. Come ON, Fixer, think!"

Fixer flew to the door, gave his wings a good flap,
and knocked on the glass with his beak, TIPPY-TAP!

Izzy got mad. "Fixer, why aren't you helping?

There's so much to fix. You're just
cawing and yelping!"

"FINE, go and play. You're no use!" Izzy cried.
She opened the door...and sent Fixer outside.

"Izzy," said Grandpa, "yes, you have things to mend,
and you need to find power, but where is your friend?

Are you certain that Fixer just wanted to play?
Go and look! You might see what he wanted to say."

Izzy watched, and remembered, feeling quite proud,
how she'd made Fixer's wings when he fell from a cloud.

He was soaring and splashing, just like a bird should.

Well, suddenly...	FINALLY, she...	UNDERSTOOD!

"Oh, Fixer! I'm sorry! We can DO it! We must!

There are just a few things that we need to adjust."

They used a glass dome.

And some paddles

and pipes!

And planks, pins, and panels of various types.

"It's noon!" said Mick Marvel. "You know what that means.
Inventors! It's time to start up your machines!"

Ignoring the thump of her heart in her chest,
Izzy pressed START...and then hoped for the best.

As Will's Opti-Logger was starting to wheeze,

Izzy and Fixer were harnessing breeze!

While fuses were blowing on Abi's Gem-Master,
Fixer tip-tapped to make their wheel faster.

As Gillian's drums all fell off,
one by one,

Izzy's machine was being
powered by sun!

And while Mick consoled
Maximilian Spout,

Izzy cheered as the shiny,
fixed tools all popped out!

"You've won first prize, Izzy!" the Professor declared.
"Oh, just look at all of these tools you've repaired!

Such a useful machine, and so well thought through, deserves not just one prize, but certainly...

TWO!"

For Mia Luna, and in memory of your sparkling Daddy, Tristan. x —P. J.

For Erika —S. O.

Published by
PEACHTREE PUBLISHING COMPANY INC.
1700 Chattahoochee Avenue
Atlanta, Georgia 30318-2112
PeachtreeBooks.com
Text © 2019 by Pip Jones
Illustrations © 2019 by Sara Ogilvie

First published in Great Britain in 2019 by Simon and Schuster UK Ltd
1st Floor, 222 Grays Inn Road, London, WC1X 8HB, A CBS Company
First United States version published in 2020 by Peachtree Publishing Company Inc.
First trade paperback edition published in 2022

The illustrations were created in pencil, ink, oil pastel, monoprint, and digital techniques.

Printed in February 2022 in China
10 9 8 7 6 5 4 3 2 1 (hardcover)
10 9 8 7 6 5 4 3 2 1 (trade paperback)
HC ISBN: 978-1-68263-164-5
PB ISBN: 978-1-68263-415-8
Cataloging-in-Publication Data is available from the Library of Congress.